Petrify

Beth Chambers

A & C Black • London

For my mother, Gaynor, and my mother-in-law, Christine. Thank you.

First published 2012 by A & C Black
an imprint of Bloomsbury Publishing Plc
50 Bedford Square London WC1B 3DP

www.acblack.com

ISBN 978-1-4081-5269-0

A CIP catalogue for this book is available from the British Library.

This book is produced using paper that is made from wood grown in managed, sustainable forests. It is natural, renewable and recyclable. The logging and manufacturing processes conform to the environmental regulations of the country of origin.

Printed by CPI Group (UK), Croydon, CR0 4YY.

Contents

Chapter 1

Ma Jessop's Woods

No one goes into the woods. No one talks about why. It's just a matter of fact. Keep out of Ma Jessop's woods.

Of course, that isn't the proper name of the woods. The proper name has faded over the years.

From the time of the first disappearance.

I have tried to make Josh understand that the woods are off limits. But he just doesn't seem to get it.

"Ooh, trees are real scary," he mocks.

I know what he's doing. Trying to wind me up so I tell him the whole story.

Well, I'm not going to fall for his trick. I look at my watch. "Teen Edge youth club opens in ten minutes," I tell him. "Do you want to hang out there for a while?"

We head along the streets to the youth club.

I push open the faded red door and Josh scoots over to the pool table.

Carrie and Helena ask me to join them.

"Who's the newbie?" Helena demands.

"Josh? He moved in next door on Tuesday."

"Cute," Carrie whistles.

Josh picks up a pool cue. He is playing against Karl, who's in my year in school.

"Nice," Karl admires as Josh pots the black.

Josh flashes Karl a grin. "Cheers mate." He gives him a high five.

"So," asks Josh, staring at me, "do you guys want to meet up tomorrow?"

"Sure." Carrie sounds keen. She *so* has a crush on Josh. "Where should we meet?"

"The woods," Josh says.

Karl scowls at me. "Ella should have told you. The woods are off limits."

"What are you afraid of? Killer rabbits?" Josh raises his eyebrows.

Helena steps in. "I don't mind going. It's not like anything is going to go wrong if we're all together."

I wait for the others to disagree but it doesn't happen. Carrie can't see beyond her crush on Josh and Karl doesn't want to look a coward.

"We'll be okay as long as we don't go too far in," says Helena. "My brother sometimes hangs out there with his mates."

"He does?" I'm surprised. It's the first I've heard of it.

"They've made a den on the edge of the woods," she tells me.

As they make plans to meet up in the morning Josh gives me a smug look.

I shake my head.

I have such a bad feeling about this.

Chapter 2

A Warning

I decide to walk home alone.

I don't even reach the end of the street when I hear the sound of footsteps running along the pavement.

"Why didn't you wait for me?" asks Josh.

I shrug. I'm still mad at him. We walk along in silence.

"Okay, I get it. You're not talking to me," Josh grumbles as we turn into our street. "You haven't said a word in the last hour."

"You want a word? How about *loser*?" I say.

Josh's eyebrows shoot up and disappear behind his messy copper fringe.

"That's a bit harsh," he mutters.

"Okay, you want to know why we never go into the woods?"

As much as I don't like him right now he deserves to be warned.

Josh's eyes light up.

"I want to know why *you* never go," he corrects me. "Helena said her brother and his mates hang out there *all the time*."

Honestly! He is so annoying.

I can't be bothered to point out that Helena's brother stays on the edge of the woods. Instead I take a deep breath.

"A couple of hundred years ago an old woman was thrown out of her village because people thought she was a witch. In the middle of the woods is an old quarry. The woman moved into the caves and tunnels of the quarry. She slept through the day and roamed the woods at night. People said she cursed anyone who came near the quarry."

I stop, unable to say the next part of the tale.

And then came the disappearances.

I press my lips together. I've said enough.

"And then what?" Josh leans forward.

My nan comes into the room carrying a teacup. Silently she rinses it at the sink. As she dries the cup she suddenly says, "It's bad luck to talk about Ma Jessop."

"Why?" mutters Josh. "She's long dead."

Nan raises her eyebrows. "They say the wickedness inside her was so strong that it stopped her growing, so she stayed the size of a child. Evil like that doesn't die easily."

"Well, it's not going to stop us going to the woods tomorrow, is it?" Josh challenges me.

I shake my head in disbelief.

"You'll bring bad luck down on you," warns Nan, giving me a worried look before leaving the room.

I almost jump out of my seat as the back door slams shut. A pane of glass breaks and shatters on the floor.

"See," I say to Josh, my voice shaking. "That's a warning."

Chapter 3

Keep Out

Once Josh has gone Nan calls me into her room. I sit on her daybed and she turns down the TV.

"There's a box under my bed," she tells me. "Get it out."

I find the small wooden box and look inside. It's full of old letters.

"Look for a necklace," Nan says.

Hidden under the letters I find a necklace made of rough wooden beads.

"I want you to have it," Nan says. "It will keep you safe when you go into the woods."

I shake my head. "I'm not going."

She leans forward and grips my hands. "You must go."

I don't understand. Only five minutes ago she was telling me not to go. Why has she suddenly changed her mind?

Nan takes the necklace and places it over my head.

"You must go," she says again. "Keep them all safe."

* * *

The next day we walk down the lane that leads to the woods. Josh is smug. He thinks I have given in. But he's wrong. I still plan to talk the others out of going.

They're all waiting. I look at Carrie's heels and short skirt. She looks like she's ready to go out to a party, not for a walk in the woods.

"Guys," I say, "I have *such* a bad feeling about this. How about we take the bus into town instead? We could go and see a film?"

Karl shrugs. "I'm broke."

"Me too," Helena agrees.

Before I can suggest anything else, Josh snatches Carrie's bag. He races along the path that leads into the woods. Carrie chases after him as fast as her heels will allow.

The others look nervous but they follow Josh anyway. I hesitate. I don't want to go into the woods. But I hear Nan's words in my mind. *Keep them safe*.

I take a deep breath and hurry along the path.

I can't see the others but I can hear them laughing. I follow the sound but they are always just out of sight.

Finally I see a glimpse of Carrie's red t-shirt. Leaving the path I scramble over rotting leaves. The sun is almost totally blotted out by the trees. My heart is thumping.

We have to get out of here.

I call out their names but there's no reply.

A flock of birds fly into the sky as I stumble into a clearing. My mouth turns dry as I realise where I am.

It's the one place I had been determined to avoid.

I'm at the entrance to the quarry.

Chapter 4

Inviting Trouble

There is something strange about the trees around the edge of the quarry. Then I get it. They all seem dead. Their branches are bare and their trunks twist away, as if they are trying to escape.

My friends are standing around the entrance to the quarry. They're looking at Josh edging into the cave.

"He's crazy!" Helena gasps as Josh disappears.

My heart starts to thump. I yell after him not to be stupid but there's no reply.

Minutes pass. I know I should go after him but my legs refuse to move.

"Josh!" Karl calls into the black opening. "Don't be an idiot. Come back."

A moment later there's a rattle of small stones and Josh appears. He grins. "Did you lot think old Ma Jessop had got me?" He waggles his fingers at me like he's casting a spell.

"You're *so* not funny," I say as Carrie squeals and throws her arms around him.

"I don't know why we were all so scared!" Helena says, moving away from the cave.

The others are quick to follow. I scowl at Josh but he whispers to me, "I've got something to show you. Come over to my house later."

* * *

It takes until three o'clock before I give in and decide to find out what Josh is talking about. I march around and bang on Josh's door.

"What did you think you were doing?" I snap as soon as he opens it.

"You know we shouldn't have gone anywhere near the quarry." My voice rises to a shout I'm so mad.

Josh grins, then he pulls out a crumpled hanky and puts it in my hands. I'm surprised by how heavy and how cold it feels. Then I realise that it's made of stone.

"Where did you get this from?" I hiss.

"Where do you think?" Josh takes the stone hanky back from me.

I should have guessed. He's taken it from Ma Jessop's caves. "You idiot!" I shout. "What have you done?"

"Get a grip, Ella!" Josh grins. "When are you going to accept there's no such thing as witches?"

I step back from him. “You’re wrong Josh. This is dangerous.”

“I’d like to see her come and get it,” he laughs.

I shake my head. I have a feeling his words may come back to haunt him.

* * *

The next morning I’m woken up by a banging on the door.

“Do you know how early it is?” I demand, as I stare at Josh.

He ignores the question. “Take it.” He pushes the stone hanky at me.

23

I stare down at the reddish brown stone. "I don't want it," I say.

Josh's voice shakes. "I couldn't sleep last night. I kept hearing noises. Freaky sounds! As if someone was trying to get in through my window..."

"Oh yeah?" I guess Josh is setting me up so he can laugh about me with the others. I bet the hanky didn't even come from Ma Jessop's cave at all.

"Take it," Josh begs. "I don't want it."

I shrug, deciding to play it cool. Even if the hanky did come from the cave it's not as if anything will happen to me.

I'm not the one that stole it.

Chapter 5

Midnight Visit

I put the stone hanky on the windowsill in my bedroom, then forget all about it as my mum takes me and Nan out for the day.

We get back late and Nan makes an excuse to get me on her own.

The moment the door shuts she asks, "Well, what happened?"

I don't tell her we went to Ma Jessop's cave. And there's no way I'm going to tell her about the hanky. Besides, the more I think about it the more I'm sure Josh is winding me up. I mean, what would Ma Jessop have wanted with a stone hanky?

"Nothing happened," I lie. "We just hung around for a while." I feel bad for not telling her the truth but I'd have felt worse if I'd made her worry.

I watch a bit of TV then I head up to bed, switch off the light and slowly drift into sleep.

I'm not sure what wakes me.

I lie in the dark, my eyes wide open, my heart thumping. The bedside clock tells me it's five past midnight. I strain my ears, but can't hear a thing. But just as my breathing slows down there's a noise directly above my bed on the roof. My mind races as I try to work out what could be making it. A branch, I tell myself, it's just a branch. The scrabbling moves in the direction of the window. Perhaps it's a bird, I think, starting to panic now. Or maybe some kind of rat or mouse?

My fingers tighten on my duvet as a horrible thought occurs to me.

The window is open.

I lie still, unable to make myself move.

Get up! Shut the window! a voice shouts in my head. The noise on the roof stops for a moment. It's long enough for me to sit up and push off my duvet. I race across the room and bang the window shut. My fingers tremble as I turn the key in the window lock.

It's pitch black outside. I can't see anything, but then, I don't want to. I turn and run back to bed.

As I pull the duvet up over my head, I hear the worst noise yet.

A screeching sound fills my room.

There's no mistaking what it is.

It's the sound of fingernails scraping against glass.

Chapter 6

Sharp Fingernails

I don't know when I fall asleep but I'm woken by birdsong. Sunlight streams through the gap in my curtains. I hurry over to the window.

It's still shut and locked and the stone hanky is exactly where I left it the day before.

Taking a deep breath I unlock my window and push it open. I lean out and stare down at the garden.

At first everything seems the same. My bike is still propped up against the fence. I can see the washing on the line. Then I stare directly below. My eyes widen as I see footprints in the soft grass. They're small, almost like a child's.

In a rush, Nan's words come back to me.

The wickedness inside her was so powerful it stopped her growing...

I shake my head. It's impossible. Sure, I believe that curses could exist, but there's no way I believe Ma Jessop's still *alive*.

My gaze moves to the stone hanky. I think back to the sound of fingernails scraping against glass.

It doesn't matter if I believe Ma Jessop is alive or not. I'm not risking another night like that. The stone hanky's going back.

Today.

I'm planning to go round to see Josh but he beats me to it. I open the door to find him standing there, his finger about to press the bell.

"How did you sleep?" he asks. "I had a much better night."

"That's because you sent all the trouble around to me," I snap.

I march up the side path and show him the footprints on the grass.

Josh hardly glances at them. Instead he stares at the fence.

"Look." He points at five scratch marks in the wooden fence. They look as if they've been made by something sharp.

"Fingernails?" I shudder.

Josh's eyebrows jerk up.

"We have to take the hanky back," I say, even though I am terrified. "Maybe then we'll be left alone?"

Before Josh can reply, the kitchen door opens and my mum calls out to us, "Come here! There's some bad news."

"Carrie and Helena went to a party last night and were in an accident on their way home," Mum tells us. "A tree fell on the roof of the car they were in."

"Oh no!" My stomach twists. "Are they going to be alright?"

Mum nods. "They're in hospital. They're going to be okay but it will be a while before they're able to come home again."

Josh and I look at each other.

"Are you thinking what I'm thinking?" he asks.

I press my lips together, feeling sick. Poor Carrie and Helena. Was this because of our visit to Ma Jessop's cave?

AMBULANC

I can't help worrying that things are only going to get worse.

* * *

Josh and I make our way through the woods without talking. When we reach the quarry Josh places the hanky at the cave's entrance.

"Aren't you going to go in?" I hiss. "So you can leave it where you found it?"

Josh's face is pale. He shakes his head.

"Do you hear that?" I grip Josh's arm. From the depths of the cave a strange sound echoes.

"Something's in there!" Josh panics.

We don't run. There's no way either of us is going to turn our back on the quarry. Instead we put one foot behind the other, walking backwards as fast as possible. Only when the quarry disappears from sight do we turn and race along the woodland trail.

"Let's hope that's worked," I gasp. "I just want life to get back to normal."

Chapter 7

Cursed

That night I sleep with my light on but all is quiet. Getting dressed the next morning I decide that taking the hanky back has worked.

Maybe now Josh will finally accept why we never go into the woods.

As I'm eating a piece of toast I get a text from Josh. My heart sinks as I read it.

`Karl's in hospital. Was attacked last night by Milo.`

"No way," I whisper. Karl's dog Milo is the dopiest animal ever. Getting out of his basket to eat his dinner was the most energy he'd spend in a day.

Nan joins me and reads the text over my shoulder. "Karl? Wasn't he with you when you went to the woods?"

My mouth is dry. "And Helena and Carrie."

Nan sits opposite me, her blue eyes serious. I tell her everything. When I say we were at the quarry she gives a little gasp. She's quiet for a while and then reaches out and covers my hand with hers.

"There's something I've never told you about the witch," she tells me. "Do you know how she kept herself alive?"

It's the worst part of the story. Ma Jessop would kidnap people and drink their blood. As she did, she would become younger and younger. I can imagine her skin getting smoother, her thin grey hair becoming thick and dark, her hunched back straightening, her lips red with blood.

"She always took young people." Nan's voice lowers. "Children... teenagers. Their blood is the most powerful, you see." Nan takes a deep breath. "It's said that, deep in the caves, water runs down the walls. If anything is left in the water it slowly turns to stone. It's called being petrified."

"The hanky," I say slowly. "The hanky was petrified."

Nan rubs her hand over her face. "The children who disappeared," she whispers. "It's said they were chained to the walls."

My stomach twists as I understand what Nan's telling me. The victims were slowly turned to stone. While still alive.

There's a knock at the front door. Josh stands there, his eyes wide with shock.

"Milo is being put down. They took him away this morning."

I shake my head, unable to speak. Karl loved that dog! I blink hard as tears fill my eyes. "We've got to do something before anything else happens..." I say, trying not to cry.

I don't finish my sentence, but I can tell Josh knows what I'm thinking.

Before anything worse happens to us.

I take Josh to Nan.

"In the past, people would leave Ma Jessop gifts at the entrance to her cave," Nan says.

"It was the only way to calm her if she became angry."

As soon as Nan goes to have a lie down, I say to Josh, "We have to go back to the quarry and leave a gift."

Josh shakes his head. "No way," he says. "I'm not going back there, ever!"

"You are," I say. "We have to. It's the only way to stop her."

Chapter 8

Stolen Gifts

When we reach the dead trees near the quarry, Josh refuses to go any further. “Why don’t you just leave the stuff here?” he asks, looking at the carrier bag I’m holding.

"You heard what Nan said," I reply. "The gift has to be left at the entrance to the cave."

Josh shakes his head and folds his arms. "I'm not going with you," he says.

I see that I'm going to have to do this alone.

My legs feel heavy as I make myself walk into the clearing. The sun is hot, making me sweat. As I get close to the cave opening it seems like a giant mouth ready to swallow me whole.

Once I reach the entrance I place the bag just inside. My heart thumps as I spin around and race back to Josh. "Let's get out of here!"

As we race in and out of the trees, I hope that the gift will be enough.

I didn't know what to leave and so in the end I chose a small silver bracelet, a bar of chocolate and a bottle of sherry.

I'm going to have some explaining to do when Mum notices they're missing.

* * *

June and half of July pass without event. The gifts seems to have done the trick.

My friends recover from the accidents, and no one suggests going into the woods again.

On the last day of school Josh invites me to go camping to celebrate the start of the summer holidays.

"Where?" I ask.

"In Crow Field," he says.

Crow Field is on the south side of the woods, but far enough away from the quarry for me to feel okay about saying yes.

Nan's not happy. "Wear the necklace," she insists.

I haven't thought about the wooden bead necklace for ages.

"The last child to disappear was over fifty years ago," Nan says. "She'll be looking for another victim one of these days."

A chill runs down my spine. It's the first time Nan has ever spoken about Ma Jessop as if she's still alive.

I remember the noise I'd heard in the caves and scrabbling over my roof.

Had that been old Ma Jessop?

"I thought she was burned at the stake," I say.

"She was," Nan replies. "But when the flames died down there was no sign of her. Not even teeth. Many people were sure she had escaped. The wooden beads on the necklace I gave you are made out of the stake Ma Jessop was tied to. She can't stand to be near them."

She holds my hands tight in hers. "Promise you'll take the necklace tonight?"

"I promise."

Chapter 9

Taken

We pitch our tents on the side of the field furthest away from the woods. When it gets dark, we make a fire and toast marshmallows while Josh starts telling ghost stories.

A bat swoops overhead as Josh says it's my turn to tell a story. "Go on," he insists.

I don't know any ghost stories, so I make one up about a vampire, a haunted castle and a lost traveller. I think it's pretty good but Josh laughs at my efforts. "Your stories suck!"

"Oh, yeah?" I've got a tale that I know will freak him out. Before stopping to question whether I'm being wise, I tell him the rest of Ma Jessop's story.

Even in the growing dark I can see Josh turn pale.

"She'd steal children and teenagers and take them deep into the quarry," I say in a low voice.

"Then she'd chain their wrists and ankles to the wall so they couldn't move. Even when they'd given up hope of being rescued and all they wanted to do was die, she would keep them alive by force-feeding them. Her victims would watch themselves turn to stone and she would drink their blood, right until they took their last breath."

Josh throws his stick onto the fire. He kicks off his boots and crawls into his tent without saying goodnight.

I feel bad for scaring him. I want to say sorry but there is no sound from Josh's tent. He's either asleep or pretending to be.

I climb into my sleeping bag in my own tent and listen to the distant bark of a fox. I reach under my pillow where I've left the necklace and slip it on. "Goodnight," I call out, just in case Josh is awake.

There's no reply and I fall asleep to the sound of grass blowing in the wind.

* * *

I'm woken by the hoot of an owl. I sit up and unzip my tent door. In the moonlight I see that Josh's tent door is also open. I creep out and see at once that Josh's sleeping bag is empty.

SNAC

"Josh?" I call.

But there is no reply and I wonder if he's legged it. All of a sudden, I feel angry. I bet he's left me here, alone.

I try to work out what to do. I can either brave out the night on my own or I can pull on my coat and shoes and run for home.

I look down at where I'd left my shoes. Beside them are Josh's boots. I stare at the boots and I know Josh would not have walked home in bare feet.

So if he hasn't gone home, where is he?

Chapter 10

Footprints

I stare out over the field. Moonlight shines down on a trail of footprints in the wet grass.

No, not one trail of footprints.

Two.

I look at the prints more closely. I've seen the small ones before.

Outside my window.

My heart thumps as I pull on my shoes and grab a torch. My hands are shaking so much that I drop it twice before I manage to switch it on. I follow the two sets of prints which lead toward the woods.

Once I leave the wet grass behind me I can't see the footprints. But it doesn't matter. I know where they're going.

I have no plan in mind as I race in the dark to the quarry. I have no idea what I'll do if I catch up with them.

Ma Jessop is alive.

The words go round and round in my head as I run through the woods, using the torch to work out which way to go. Every sound makes me more and more afraid. I scare a bird out of a nearby bush and cry out with fright as it flaps away, brushing my face with its wing.

It's much harder finding my way in the dark. I stumble over half-hidden stones and wander off the track into thorny brambles.

Finally, I find the clearing and call out, "Josh! Are you there?"

I reach the quarry entrance but I can't make myself go into the pitch-black tunnels and caves.

"Josh!" I yell out one more time before pulling out my mobile phone. Then I do what I should have done when I first noticed Josh was gone.

I dial 999.

Chapter 11

A Promise

Weeks go by. The police search the woods and the quarry for Josh but can't find any sign of him. They question me over and over again. But it's clear that they don't believe my story.

I can hardly sleep at night. I keep thinking about what might be happening to Josh. No one believes me. Not even my friends, even though they join in local search parties and spend weeks hunting for Josh.

But in the end we have to give up. We have to admit he has disappeared without trace.

I blame myself. Nan tells me I shouldn't, but I was with him when he was taken. I look in the mirror and ask myself, "Why did she choose him instead of me?"

When I ask Nan the same question, she tells me it's the wooden beads on the necklace that saved me.

"I told you," Nan says. "Ma Jessop can't stand being near the wood that came from the stake she was tied to. She can feel the flames all over again."

The more I think about it the more I believe Nan. After all, the witch didn't come in through my open bedroom window when she had the chance.

I know there's only one way to prove my theory. I have to go to the quarry, and this time I have to go inside the caves.

I don't tell anyone where I'm going. My parents are so frightened by Josh's disappearance that they won't let me anywhere near the woods anymore.

As I make my way to the quarry I can't believe that Josh has been missing for the whole summer. I reach up for the necklace and my fingers tighten over the wooden beads. Suddenly I hear the rumble of thunder and it starts to rain. I am soaked to the skin in seconds and can't stop myself shivering.

I switch on my torch and step into the cave. I feel like I can hardly breathe as I shuffle forward. After just a few minutes I reach a dead end. There is nothing here and nowhere left to go.

As I turn to leave, the torch light picks out a narrow opening that I'm sure wasn't there a moment ago.

I don't want to go any further but I know I have to see where this tunnel goes.

I force myself to crawl through the tunnel and into another cave. I straighten up, and scream as I see two eyes glinting in the darkness. I jump back and bang my head against the wall. The torch falls to the ground and goes out.

Dropping onto my knees, I feel around in the dark until I finally grasp the torch. I shake it and sob in relief as the light flashes back on. Then I see the staring face of a teddy bear.

A stone teddy bear.

I force myself to look around the cave, and I find a huge collection of stone hankies, toys, bags and shoes.

These things once belonged to Ma Jessop's victims. I feel sick and press my hand over my mouth.

Suddenly I become angry instead of scared. I take a deep breath and yell Josh's name out as loud as I can.

I listen hard but there's no reply.

Shaking with fear and rage, I realise that I can't do any more and I turn to go. It's then that I hear a reply so faint I wonder if I've imagined it.

"Ella!"

"Josh?" I yell again, but this time nothing comes back.

Did I really hear him?

I hold out the necklace and begin to shout. "You hate this, don't you, Ma Jessop? It reminds you of the time you burned. The time when you got to feel a little of the pain that you deal out to others. Well, listen up. If you don't let Josh go then I'll come back. I'll come back again and again until he comes home. I'm not scared of you any more, you witch! But I'll make you scared of me. Do you hear?"

The words boom around the cave, following me as I feel my way back down the tunnel and towards the light.

I step out of the cave and look back. "Come back, Josh," I whisper. "Come home soon."

Chapter 12

As Good as Dead

Starting school without Josh is weird. As I walk down the street I remember how he used to annoy me by talking too much. Now the walk to school is boring.

And lonely.

Nothing's happened since I went to the cave. Yesterday I told Nan what I'd done. She gripped my hand and her eyes had tears in them as she whispered, "I'm proud of you, Ella."

In school no one talks about Josh. It's as if he's dead. Everyone wants to act as if Josh never existed but I can't do that.

He's my best friend. And best mates never give up on each other.

I drag myself through the day until it's time to go home. When I turn into my street the first thing I notice is the police car parked outside Josh's house. As I get closer I see a crowd of people holding microphones and cameras.

The moment I reach my house they turn on me.

"Do you know the missing boy?"

"Are you Josh's friend?"

"How did you feel when you heard..."

I slam the front door behind me, shutting out their questions. I drop my bag and race to the kitchen where Mum and Nan are sitting at the table. They turn to me and I can see they have both been crying. Mum dabs at her eyes. "They've found Josh," she says with a sob.

I feel my legs start to buckle under me. I can't help thinking the worst.

He's dead, he's been found, cold and alone and dead.

"Ella," sobs Mum. "He's alive!"

I want to go around to see him but I'm not allowed. So I make one last trip back to the quarry. This time I take the wooden necklace and hang it over the entrance of the cave. That should stop any more night visits from old Ma Jessop.

* * *

It takes days before the reporters move away from outside Josh's house. At school suddenly everyone wants to talk about him. Now I'm the one who goes quiet when his name is mentioned.

Josh finally comes back to school on a rainy October day. The clouds are grey and there's a cold chill in the air.

Josh is late and he sits at the back of the class on his own. He won't look at anyone even though everyone's staring at him. He looks different. His skin is pale and his hair has grown long so it reaches his shoulders. But it's his eyes that have changed the most. It's as if there is no one there. As if the Josh I used to know is dead.

By the end of the day people have given up trying to talk to him. I've already got into a fight with Karl because he called Josh a freak.

Josh doesn't wait to walk home with me and so I have to run to catch him up.

"Josh, wait up," I call as I race after him.

Josh just keeps walking slowly. He doesn't say a word. He won't even look at me. It's as if he's locked inside his own world and doesn't know what's going on around him.

"I went back for you," I tell him. "I told her I'd keep coming back until she let you go." My words tumble out. "I can't believe it worked and you're safe! She won't hurt you ever again, Josh. I've made sure..."

My voice tails off as Josh ignores me.

It's as if I'm invisible.

He just keeps walking with heavy steps, staring ahead with empty eyes. As I gaze after him there's a sudden gust of wind. It blows his hair away from his neck. I stare in horror at the reddish brown stone where there should have been skin.

Part of him has been turned to stone.

Josh has been petrified.